MAX

MAX

story & pictures by
Rachel Isadora

Aladdin Paperbacks

Aladdin Paperbacks
An imprint of Simon & Schuster
Children's Publishing Division
1230 Avenue of the Americas
New York, NY 10020

First Aladdin Paperbacks edition, 1987
Also available in a hardcover edition from
Simon & Schuster Books for Young Readers
Manufactured in China
30
Library of Congress Cataloging in Publication Data
Isadora, Rachel.
Max.
Reprint. Originally published: New York: Macmillan,
1976.
Summary: Max finds a new way to warm up for his
Saturday baseball game—his sister's dancing class.
[1. Dancing—Fiction. 2. Baseball—Fiction]
I. Title.
PZ7.I763Max 1984   [E]   84-7649
ISBN 978-0-02-043800-7 (pbk.)
0918 SCP

For my parents
and Grandfather Max

With special thanks to
Libby, Alan,
and of course, Brian

Max is a great baseball player. He can run fast, jump high, and hardly ever misses a ball. Every Saturday he plays with his team in the park.

On Saturday mornings he walks with his sister Lisa to her dancing school. The school is on the way to the park.

One Saturday when they reach the school, Max still has
lots of time before the game is to start. Lisa asks him
if he wants to come inside for a while.

Max doesn't really want to, but he says O.K. Soon the class begins. He gets a chair and sits near the door to watch.

The teacher invites Max
to join the class, but he must
take off his sneakers first.

He stretches at the barre.

He tries to do the split.

And the pas de chat. He is having fun.

Just as the class lines up to do leaps across the floor,
Lisa points to the clock. It is time for Max to leave.

Max doesn't want to miss the leaps. He waits
and takes his turn.

Then he must go.

He leaps all the way to the park.

He is late. Everybody is waiting for him.

He goes up to bat.

Strike one!

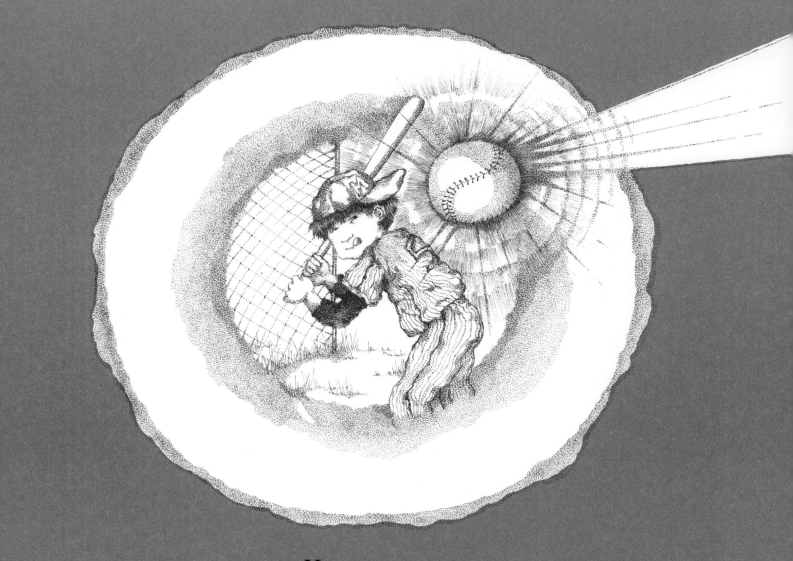

He tries again.

Strike two!

And then...

A home run!